T0132334

SHADOWUS

Linda Joyce

AuthorHouse™
1663 Liberty Drive
Bloomington, IN 47403
www.authorhouse.com
Phone: 1 (800) 839-8640

Published by AuthorHouse 06/17/2019

ISBN: 978-1-7283-1594-2 (sc)
ISBN: 978-1-7283-1595-9 (e)

Library of Congress Control Number: 2019907787

Print information available on the last page.

This book is printed on acid-free paper.

authorHOUSE®

Shadowus was born in Paradoxy the moment the day went dark and the moon crossed in front of the sun. He was the first son born to King Larrius and Queen Joyus who were the rulers of Paradoxy. Shadowus was born with a strange black form that lay on the ground beside him. No one in Paradoxy, including the king and queen had ever seen anything like this before.

The king and queen didn't know what royal title Shadowus should have so they decided to take Shadowus to Albertius, the wisest man in Paradoxy. Albertius told them it was a question-able mystery and as black as the form was, it was baby Shadowus's aura and was likely to continually change and would work itself out in the end.

As Shadowus grew, his ever-changing black aura also grew with its many changing shapes and designs that followed him everywhere he went.

Sometimes the black form grew to be as big as a bear!

Shadowus felt like a frog instead of a prince. He wished to have his black aura changed into a beautiful shiny, sparkly aura and to wear a beautiful crown like the other royalty in Paradoxy.

Shadowus hated the ugly black spot on the ground that followed him everywhere! He wanted to change his shadow into something beautiful! He went to see Denisus, the artist of the rainbow, to have his shadow painted with splendid iridescent colors. Denisus painted the ground where Shadowus stood.

When her painting was finished Shadowus stepped out of a painted garden but still had his black form attached like a puppy at his heels.

His black aura could not be painted!

Shadowus then went to Seanus and Brandorius, the twin princes of the sea, thinking he could wash the black aura away. As the twin princes handed him the best soaps from the sea, he watched a seahorse form and blow bubbles in the salt water.

When Shadowus came out of the water his black aura had not been washed away, the black form stood like a flamingo on the shore awaiting his exit from the water.

The black aura would not wash away!

Shadowus went to Patorius, the prince of swiftness and they tried to out run it! Shadowus ran as swift as a deer

but the black aura only ended up a hare in front of him at the finish line!

He could not outrun the black aura!

He went to Victorius, the prince to the big winds. Victorius blew his big winds as strong as a twisting tornado. No matter how hard the winds blew,

The black aura would not blow away!

He went to see Peteronius, the prince to the sky's lightning bolts, and tried to bury the black form in the ground. They used Peteronius' lightning bolts like shovels as they dug from the light side of day to the dark side of night, until they dug a black hole all the way through Paradoxy!

When they finished both stood back to look through the black hole they had dug and saw the moon taking a nap, just before it prepared to set out for the evening.

Shadowus could not bury his black aura!

He went to see Mikus, the prince of the sun's rays. They each grabbed torches from Mikus's crown and tried to burn it away.

But when the smoke cleared all that remained was a black forest!

The black aura would not burn away!

Shadowus was finally exhausted from all he had tried and was on his way home. Along the way he met Sunni, Misty, Shauna and Julie, the four skylight princesses, the princesses to all light reflections in the world. After Shadowus explained what he had been doing all day to rid himself of his black aura, they all tried to cut the black form away!

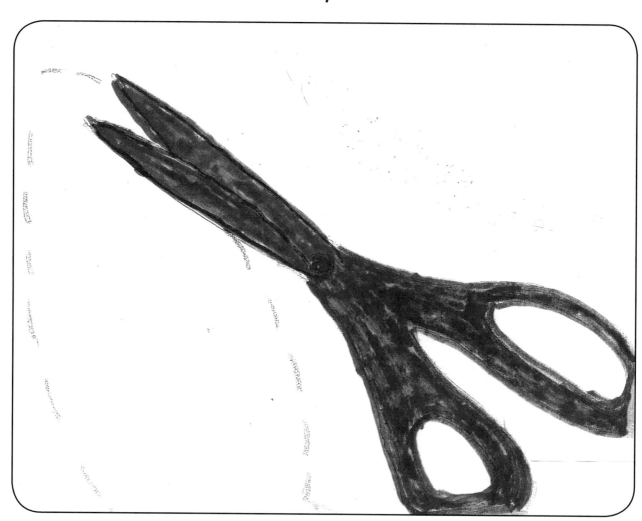

When they all cut together they successfully separated the black aura from Shadowus! When the cutting was done, it was no longer attached to him.

They had cut away the black aura!

The skylight princesses and Shadowus carried the black aura to the black hole dug clear through Paradoxy and tossed it into the hole.

They watched it get smaller and smaller as it fell, until it became like

a shooting star that disappeared somewhere into space.

Shadowus hurried to show everyone that his black aura was gone. He pointed down to the ground to the empty spot where there was nothing!

Shadowus was excited to tell everyone his black aura was gone!

Pegtoria, the princess of all knowledge told Shadowus it was a definite requirement for all in Paradoxy to have an aura of some kind. Shadowus would have to leave Paradoxy to go find and re-unite with his aura and only then could he come back to Paradoxy.

Then Shadowus wanted nothing more than to have his great aura back! He went back to the black hole dug through Paradoxy and stood at its edge.

The black hole sucked him in like a vacuum. He took off into space. He twirled and twisted in the heavens and disappeared just like his black aura had done.

He was spit out from the black hole behind the sun and found himself in a strange place. It was the planet of gravity that had pulled him in like a magnet.

He noticed that everything there had a black form of its own. Some forms were small, some were big, some were fat, some were skinny and some were tall, but he noted that everything and everyone on the planet of gravity had one.

Shadowus searched everywhere on the planet of gravity for his black aura.

He eventually met a tall tree that told him it had seen a shooting star land with a splash into the lake.

Shadowus could see a black form swimming like a fish at the bottom of the lake.

He dove down, grabbed the black form, jumped on its back and rode up to the surface like a boy riding a dolphin. As he came to the lake's shore, he wrapped the black form around himself like a large beach towel.

Shadowus noticed a surfboard floating in the ocean. He grabbed the surfboard's black form and ran quickly towards the sun before it set.

He used the surfboard's black form as a surfboard to paddle his way towards the setting sun. He made it just as the sun was setting behind the black hole behind the sun that had sucked him into it like a vacuum.

He took off into space riding his black aura like a speeding rocket in a hurry to get back home to Paradoxy.

Shadowus was spit out of the black hole and went flying through the air like a bird. He landed right in the painted garden Deniseus had painted with bright colors. When he landed in the painted garden he knew he was home again, and his black aura had re-united with him and attached to him like a turtle to its shell.

Shadowus hurried back to tell the royal family about his adventures on the planet of gravity, how everything there had a black aura of its own. Princess Joanna, the princess of all light, stepped forward to ask Shadowus to share what he had learned from his experience. He explained to everyone that sometimes we do not realize the gifts we have until we lose them and that his black aura was a gift from the sun to remind him he was not alone in the world!

Everyone gathered around as Christorius, the christening prince, stepped forward to christen Shadowus with his title. The king and queen crowned Shadowus with a tall golden crown. Christorius conferred with King Larrius and Queen Joyus and decided they would call his black aura a shadow and give him the title of Prince Shadowus, a prince to watch over all the shadows in the world!

All the Royal Family in Paradoxy gathered together with Shadowus as he stood proudly with his beloved shadow, happy he was not alone in the world. Princess Joanna of all light stepped back from the group with her celestial camera. With her perfect light, Princess Joanna made sure the sun was sitting just right as she said to all......

Smile everybody because the sun is shining

its gifts on all of us today!

sun and me

(Dedicated to my son, Chris)

Printed in the United States
By Bookmasters